"A captivating allegorical novella about the death of conscience and diminutive puppet-like roles of people in a corrupted world. Guaranteed to stir the core of the human soul."

Vatsala Radhakeesoon (Mauritian author/poet)

—

"A wonderful piece of writing. Dunn's lucid and musical prose seeps into your consciousness and lingers, just the right mix of genuine lyricism and delirious imagery. Sitting on the Floor is open-wounded. It should come with sutures."

Jeff Bowles, author of *God's Body*

Sitting on the floor

Robin Wyatt Dunn

By Robin Wyatt Dunn

POETRY

Poems from the War
Science Fiction: a poem!
Sunsborne
Wine Country
What Black Delirious Daylight Sets You Forward in the Boat
Remarriages
Debudaderrah
Black Heart Uprising

NOVELS

Los Angeles, or American Pharaohs
My Name is Dee
Fighting Down into the Kingdom of Dreams
Line to Night Island
A Map of Kex's Face
Julia, Skydaughter
Conquistador of the Night Lands
White Man Book
Colonel Stierlitz
Black Dove
City, Psychonaut
2DEE
Now the last light
This isn't one of the stories I remember
The Black King of Kalfour

By Robin Wyatt Dunn

SHORT STORIES
Dark is a Color of the Day

PLAYS
Last Freedom

FILMS
A Wilderness in Your Heart
Party Games
American Messenger

JOHN OTT
SAN DIEGO, CALIFORNIA
2019

ISBN - 978-1-940830-30-8
LOC - 2019904882

Cover art by Barbara Sobczyńska

for Saira Viola

Part 1

1.

Sitting on the floor I realized how long I'd been away—it hadn't been long, only a few months or years, but it felt like a long time. One wonders how long the years have been keeping away like this—whether in fact I've been counting them correctly. I'm not sure what day it is—perhaps Thursday—and the week has been going so incredibly well I hardly know what to do. I don't think I'm used to things going well.

We'll hear the reasons in time, perhaps; but now I don't want to know them. It's enough to be here, waiting for the end of them, in the silence of the week, saintly and uninterrupted, writing.

I won't know but I can guess:

She came in through the door wearing yellow, shouting at something she'd seen crawling over the wall, demanding answers, beating the floor with her fists in a sexy way, shaking her hair around her head like a miasma of networked nodes, competing for space, fighting for money, deliverance, authenticity, pain, love, recognition, reality.

She's both real and not. Like me.

We'll begin in the ordinary way: I was born a man and this is my testimony. Except I wasn't born a man I was born a boy. Born male. But maleness is not manhood. And in becoming a man one keeps the boy too. This is my testimony, boy-man.

Man-boy. Written in the event of my coming to be, again.

We are arrived and this is the music, not yet here, but arriving, with me, who should befriend this audience with your likelihood—your removal—your certain event so we may listen and decide just what it is to do.

Who are you, doing? Which are you, making. Upright and shallow and full of verve. We have your number. We're making it tick. We're making it ours.

Write the number on the page—one, two, three, and press:

Press in. Press in and wait, for the moment to the edge, of being: not without removal, nor the circumspection of your allowances, so sure to know, to remain, like English noblemen in their chattel and charnel houses. Raking in the leaves. Spitting in the profits.

We're marking in in the department. Lean in better so we may hear you, sir. We're rolling.

Set in and fear, man, for your mine is ours, ruckussed and subsumed ornery galactic, to weather with our bearances the need and want of us, so true because we're beating you.

Well, What else is there to say.

I believe I am coming to a place where I no longer need you to agree. What a child I was. Perhaps in time I will no longer even need to explain.

That time is not yet here but I can imagine it might arrive.

The enactment itself: *who heard it best*

The enchantment itself: *all of our bodies*

The renunciation itself: *we're going down*

Go down into the depths with me, and though we shall not return we shall be better for it, as a quantum mechanics equation, kitty kitty kitty kitty kitty sweet sweet kitty lonely and sold, waiting for your package to be delivered . . . here kitty kitty

Here kitty kitty. Here kitty kitty here is the message. All stars are far away. All nights are near. We're weathering the bearances; watching the receding stars, needing one another tonight and for quite some time, to administer the repackaging of our awareness into new equations, no longer entirely Schrödinger's.

O Schrödinger, you smorgasbord and goomba. We'll deliver you too. I promise.

Come down, under the earth.

Come down into Gobekli Tepe, and deeper, down under the Silver Chair and the juicy diamonds Lewis found (all of those Lewises!) over the continents of the mind.

Tell me what it is we know. Who made the earth and why, and which continents arose when, and for what reasons. And all of their many Gondwalla names.

The Stylite knows the answer: it is in singularity

that one achieves communion, but in achieving it, in biting at that bright berry, one can tend to confuse yourself for others, and others for yourself. It's not needful to explain, or even separate, but the question is which amalgamation which will become dominant.

We are all possessed. All these bequeathements of demons who are our ancestors. Demons are only souls and spirits, you know. Hungry like you and me. Wanting attention. Needing answers.

You are possessed by the you of both yesterday and tomorrow, so you're this slippage in the gap, desperately attaching yourself to the steel poles of the bus, as it jerks itself into the express lane of the freeway:

We're going down. Down under Galacticus and Los Angeles, down under New York and London and Abu Dhabi, down under the gales and breeze, into the mind of the earth.

Step one and two, three and four, and five, come down, my lullaby, come down, under the earth, we're going down, one, two, three, four, five, six, seven:

Count them with me, around the meditating spiral stone earth and loam, bearing our passage out of the past (just like in the noir!) and towards this deliverance (just like the movie!) who may be bloody but necessary, this bearance and joinance and hysteresis we elide under the map of now.

Can you map now? Well, no, and me neither. Nevertheless the map exists, in language. This surface tension of the ocean over which the birds levitate a bit, saving energy for the trip home.

In the bright skully daytime beneath the earth, we are seeking answers, like the agoraphobic and thoroughly paranoid characters of some Asimov novel, married to science and each other, and determined to do battle with the forces of the universe using the only tool we know: our mind. And like Asimov's characters this is already our greatest mistake, since in becoming married to our own minds we forget about others. Always this system of relations.

Still, it's beautiful, isn't it? Look around at all these old 1950s and 1960s and 1970s stereotypes of the future world: the bright white columns and the homey atmosphere and the Greco-Roman robes and the terrible secrets, here beneath the earth:

Here where so many of our ancestors sacrificed children. Cut their throats and ate their flesh, so they could name themselves gods.

Asimov never included those parts. Too hot for TV.

We're too hot for TV; burning up. I'm too hot for TV, baby. I need you to cool me off. Give me your mouth.

One two. One.

All the old men and the young women (no coincidence there!) and a few of the studs around, for attention. To make that new world. To pledge allegiance to the (god/ constitution/ ancestor). To dance slow around the firelight and sleep, first in our mind, and second in our body.

Sleep with me, underneath the hand of god, pressing down, pushing in, looking for treasure, looking for meaning, looking for the right answer to a non-existent equation, rubbing in the blood and salt, and lurking under the dog parlor for the biscuit, naming everything he can see everything she can see, naming the world with fervent delight, oligarch of names, ritual enactor of liturgical dawn, slam hammy and slack, O slack and main, O stark and servitude remain my oath, lingering long to die beneath our beautiful tomb.

2.
Gobekli tepe

The light summons everything; I can hardly see.

First the animals must be cut up; there are a great many of them and the people expect it to be done, even though I have no stomach for it.

We're working to outlive ourselves, to move to a time underneath time where we will not be accountable for our actions or futures, and I fear we have succeeded.

Somehow the blood does it: moves us deeper into this reverie we can't escape.

I open the lamb and gaze into the audience's eyes; I am the sacrificial lord.

- -

Woman in yellow, fresh from the sunrise, without token or remembrance, unutterable. In our sacrifices we require a cipher, a woman, to move through our ceremony and so provide, if not a reason, then the focus for our work. For men, killing for women makes sense. But the deeper meaning is one of our hijacked temporality, unable to divorce our human minds from the forms they have taken, until death. In providing death, we hover near to our own exits.

Woman in yellow, color of madness, arbiter card kept dull and faint noxious yellow; love. Woman in yellow of madness, stark raving main, ope thy mouth for the meat.

It's a good meal and a good sunrise; people have come from all around, as we've been doing for centuries. In the light we are transformed from creatures of darkness into shadows, hovering over the faint movements of the air. Flickering like heat in flame. I kiss her lips and taste the blood.

I raise my arm and my men and I dance. Moving through the blood.

O eidolon mine, dream self under my head, shake my arm and make me sing. Bind me to this earth. O welt and flame.

"Are we still going to do it?" she asks me.

Yes. But I don't know when. I don't know when to leave.

Who makes the lake expand, blood on the sand and thoughts in my mind, dripping over the deep black expanse of time, rigid honorific: sir master slave and wren, into the den of the king rat mane, augurer and life jump:

Jump and slip under the sea above the waves:

3.

We can't know our own ends but we can know others. The dancing yellow woman wants us all to die; I know this about her. She worships death and wants it to come for all of us. She is demented; it's why I love her. Perhaps one day she will snap because her dream has not come true. Until then, she is the most beautiful thing on the hill.

Watch the long lock of time—her ardent rue and matched paper break stone and shake churning before us—this long lance of our desire—I know some part of it, beating closer. Beating closer to me, reasons unknowable, but shocking those things deeper than reasons up to the surface of my skin—emergent galaxies.

They are herding the new crop of goats over into the grass. One of the shepherds eyes me with hate, and burnt love. We're making the world new; so new I can hardly recognize it.

"You need to cut your hair," she says.

"Cut it for me then."

She makes as though to cut my throat and I smile wide into her face, and her eyes stun the light around her head.

One hour or two; we're eating some of the cheese.

One mirror or two; like my priest is mapping the routes of the dead under the ground.

The earth has been getting drier; we have been

praying for rain. In many ways I no longer care if our colony is destroyed; the work has already been done. We will spread from here and remake every wood and land we find.

4.

The light expands over my head; under the drug. It is a mistake to believe that experience of drugs is contained within the plant compounds we make. Rather they are resonators; crystal receivers. Like the priest's map of the temples in other countries; we remember the routes both underground and in the sky.

I am journeying to Canopus to offer a gift to the gods.

Overhead, the stars approach my eyes. I close my lids and go into the arms of the blue sun.

5.

Wish whack and moan; herd the silent ocean under the drum whose awe and raft shall becalm thy soul; no other reason for it; no other shelter. Build the wrack duff and music new; wrack weal and mark the minute; mark the maely minute for the truer curve under your slippery arm;

Which vale or tumble will we embrace; red green and churning; which man am I become?

Already I am returned but also I have not left; as I had afeared, and my father too—I am split.

No, split is not the right word. Doubled. I am double-being near the arm of the god of Canopus, and in my woman's arms.

She is bringing me back to life; I vomit blood.

We are making love in the grass.

Wear and redeem; herd harsh and fail bright my lackey leering lackey hungry loom voluminous starry shroud and shake; take me into your arms.

Like a baby I howl to make sure I live.

They say I am a keeper but this is not a keep. We are only direction finders. I am only a point; like a dog. I will scent and show the direction of the sound.

Each node in the network of our dead demands sacrifice; and I do it gladly, though it kills me. If I die enough I will be permitted to rest under the ground; but not yet.

I am not coming yet; soon.

Who will I be, father?

6.

We're moving north into the winter grounds.

"Caribou, Deerblack." He calls me by my hunting name.

I smile at him and hold his shoulder. I am young but am growing weaker. It may be I will teach his son the way of traveling in the stars; he knows this and is afraid.

"Shall I hunt with you?"

"Pray for us instead."

It is as though I am already dead.

Who watches the steed and the weight; who herds the light? Who makes light come? Which death and girth, numinous arboring mast; whose growling face makes me want more? It's me; the other me. My brothers. There are too many words for the thing; and not enough. I wish I had never learned these prayers.

7.

We're drumming.

One four and seven; four hundred and ninety five; eight hundred and sixty two; nine thousand.

We're passing
Surpassing
Which arm and war
Which girl
Which horror
I will transmit it
We're drumming

This is the legacy of my birthright; each black name on the wall (later a scroll). This is the come-uppance.

8.

"Do you think you have not been watched?"

"I don't know brother."

"We know everything you do here."

I say nothing.

"Return to your box."

I go back under the deer skin and wait. Brownstaff does not trust me.

"The man should be punished," Brownstaff says. "He is disgusting."

"You do it then," says Leerfoot.

But he does not do it. They leave me under the deerskin for five hours. Perhaps that is the punishment. I hear every word but only understand one in ten. I am initiate.

9.

Has it ever happened to you that many things happen at once, both in the future and past? This is what is happening to me.

I am with my wife (she claims we are not married, but everyone knows we are). I am with the brothers too, when I was young and in training.

Canopus is here too, somewhere nearby.

Perhaps it does not matter. Is it necessary for me to distinguish between them? Perhaps Canopus will tell me. But I know I must decide for myself.

10.

Cold the face of the woman; gnarr the face of the woman; weapon mine, wash weight and marry the burial rite of love; no truer gesture; each inhabitant a lightning filled wind. I am inside my woman over the grass.

One day I will be dead—one day soon. The keeper of the writing will mark my name into the wall with charcoal, next to all the others. My movements in her are like the movements of his hand with the coal. Making sure it is accurate. Legible. Worthy of remembering.

What acid wash mercurial vise weary heart? How shall we recite the meaning underneath the shade of your eyes? Who made them so mad? Was it me? I don't think so but I it could have been. Wait for the orange dust; hear each bell; blacker day; summer night; shackle your body onto the stone as we do our food; wait for the window in the sky to harmonize with thee; lore and love; what righteous dancer were you first when I saw you?

What dead thing; broken into the waves of trees, incorruptible?

Who murders me tonight; to bury me in the sky?

11.

What word—who hears it?—which match and frame, which terror and which dream, narcowrit and fluttered over your head—which rush and whose neck, whose hill? Whose Potbelly Hill? Whose world is this, sunning under?

"   " she says.

And I say "shhhhhhhhh :

Shh under the horizon all unknown, when winter is done we'll return, making the parrots speak in a new language, and making new sureties against your dreams, investing in wind and solar, the storm and the sea.

Invest in me; narcowriter. Each death I write remembers the evening and the sound of it, remembers the beaten edge of the pavement, the emblem of the world, no never nearer, not hereafter, but not now, so soon; sooner than anything—almost happening—nearer than sound—creasing your helmet into the whiling maw of it, at home.

We're at home; it is unstoppable; unstoppable home; royal hinterland; Escher in the Mayflower; bent underneath the sun.

12.

Give me the drug and I'm grateful for it; I never meant it anyway; there was no reason for it; no fundamental expression. I was willing to sail anywhere; do anything; name anyone; kill and be betrayed, storm the barricades and die; elucidate the finest points of monopoly, monarchy and generational cruelty at daggerpoint; sing.

I was willing to sing all of it.

Willing to collude with all of it. Deck the halls with images and faces, songs, pictures and stories of our great and beautiful lies; each lie more beautiful than the last. Pasting my face with them. Expensive makeup.

Going out into the cold, like into a nuclear winter, to summon the sun, tasting the snow.

Give me the drug again, Violin, and cello. I will not argue; not retreat; I will say nothing. I will do anything you ask; I will not falter, nor retreat, I will be grateful to bury you with me in the earth, so near to my lips and hands.

Give me the drug again, cello, and I will swirl the world about in my hand, a wizard, and deliver it to you for dinner.

Come with me and my wizardry down into the dark.

These are our torture rooms where we keep the victims so their sounds can be heard above, to terrify the population.

Here is my book where I record the methods used on the bodies of the unfortunates.

This is my crystal ball, where I listen for the sounds from beyond this earth.

And here is my heart, beating out of my chest, needing you, near me, so I can remember I am a human being.

This is my journey out of this life and into the next; and it will be yours too. We are recorded in language; every bereft death. Every moment of suffering. Every hope. Every problem with no solution.

What we don't record well is dreams, and that is why I have begun this narrative which will damn me.

13.

We invest in the end: a nostalgia for the present. It's a bit like selling your present out from under you: a mortgage. It's there in the word, isn't it? That deadening. Bringing death closer to kiss.

We push the present into absence so we can grow fonder. And then we sing about it.

But in singing about it we also invite it back in, changed. The not-future not-past not-present that is present in the music. We invite it in for dialogue. Like talking to god.

God, this is some real shit you got here. What in the fuck is this shit.

God's not sure either.

He's just as curious as we are.

In the distribution of awareness we come upon the problem of invitation; the problem of the party; who is invited?

Who is invited to the party.

Down below.

Step careful; we can go pretty deep.

Kiss the doorkeeper on his cheek.

Who is invited?

Who will keep the keep and make our music pitch into forever?

Who is invited?

What kind of person is invited.

My invitation is an invitation to worthlessness. Discard as much as you can—not everything, but as much as you can—and then reassess, like in the worst and most derivative self-help book you can imagine, all the truths of your life.

Who is it hurt you?

Who made you come?

What did you think you were doing when you took that first step? Even if you were a child you still decided. It was something you did. You were curious. Just like god. Just like me. Just like this music, pulsing underneath us. Demanding that we demonstrate our allegiance to its insurgent energy, unstoppable. If we give in to the music, we are lost. Yet I believe that may be why I have invited you, as a kind of evil accompaniment to my own exit from all that I knew; I will feel better if I bring someone with me.

I'm sorry. It's wrong, but that doesn't matter now. You're here too.

We're going.

14.

She's watching the rain. It's falling over the cows and into the furrows. The world is empty before us, like a great whirlpool, waiting to suck us in.

She turns to look at me with her almost-black eyes. I smile at her and she's looking for something in my face; something I don't know what it is.

I no longer know what it is I've become.

15.

Of course a doomed story is beautiful; because this means it is already over before it is begun. No story is truly like this; no story can begin or end. We make it end; and the doomed story, being ended twice, is doubly satisfying.

What else could we do in anticipation of the end, than fall in love? It invites it immediately, with no presaged thought or word, an illustrated love affair of sound, bent under the winter of our civilization, and those things which were civilization long before we had cities.

In the end, or in approaching it, we are reborn.

It is better to end at the beginning, then, since we can come to the story with no preconceptions or worries, other than that of the baby: food, shelter, and clothing. Is it then so different?

Even the baby is worried, isn't he?

Bent under the swell of the sun, we're diadem-crouching under the starless wastes, the mood and blasted catacombs of the stars, no one can say their names—

Who is it here? Tell us, just how it will end again. Tell us again, which moons and stars blew us apart, which dreams were shattered, and which loves were consummated in flame.

Consummate me in flame, love, for I am dead, and this story is about death, and the feeling before it. We see it coming, our deeper love, with the changing universe, and this fear breaks our hearts, and builds it up again, in the knowledge of our terrible history and flame, no truer representation of love than in the approaching death (and this why Keats was so great a poet).

Well, you know all this. What I am trying to understand is why I went on this way: watching the end at the height of my life, in full knowledge of its incapacitating splendor, luxuriating in the power of the expression of the universe as designed, for a man, designed to kill you. Like the deer in the headlights.

They come on slow over us, on potbelly hill. Those great headlights swirling down:

16.

Skipping over the lights, into the flame; redolent of Sunday and crème brulee; swimming deeper in:

"Why don't you make love to me any more?"

We're flying in space.

We're not dreaming Sunday

It's dreaming us

We're not living today

We're living tomorrow

Under the headache of time

Summoned singing

"Oh God! What is it!"

"Shhh. It'll pass."

They say outer space is like a drug experience. But my question is: what's the difference?

"Who is it listening?" she whispers in my ear.

"It's no one."

The black night is swirling around us.

There is some tension between everything I have known and what experiences have come to be mine since I was elected ruler of Gobekli Tepe; but no, that is wrong.

It is rather that I do not properly exist; and in our visitations outside of this earth we are meeting some of the things we are slowly coming to be.

- -

I am not dead; I have been lying. But the thing of it is that I want to be; and this desire of mine complicates my relationship to life. It is not that it makes it maudlin or dreary; rather it excites me, and I crave life all the more, in my knowledge of its immanent and imminent endliness; *endlich mein herr*, there is no other; no other reason.

It is fine for Caesar to revel in his pronouncements; but that was then and this is now—rather, before. Caesar benefited from all of my decisions. He already knew what was coming: I was. This thing we made here. This unbelievable thing.

I can't say *veni vidi vici*—the only true part, or partly true part, of that for me is *vidi*, but rather it is *coming to see. Almost seen. Something I might be able to see, if only I can find the name for it.*

This wasn't Caesar's problem. So of course I'm jealous. Jealous of all that is to happen.

But maybe we do have the same problem after all:

The problem of supremacy. Supremacy and survival share the common root of uper: overhead, above. Last man standing.

The problem of supremacy is the problem of survival. By its very nature there is no question of ethics: whatever you did helped you to be alive now, and so it must have been good.

I am not dead; nor is this a desirable state. I am undead; outside of time. Like god, under the influence of our drug.

Give me the night; and I will give you this story, of our journey out from Gobekli Tepe into Iraq and Syria, into this terrible thing we made.

I am not sorry that we made it. It was something necessary; it still is. Nor was it entirely of my doing, obviously. But we decided that it was good. To see our neighbors from the sky, and our neighbors on the ground, and come to communion with them, here in the nightmare that is our new civilization.

17.

"Do you think I might be dead?" she asks.

"We both are, my lovely."

"Oh."

"And we're coming to be."

"Oh god."

I touch her wet cunt, like the sea shells over Lebanon.

We're coming to be, I know it; better than I have ever known anything. What else could be more certain? Death is nothing in the face of certainty—the most powerful illusion that exists.

I buy her falafel under the canopy of the truck man in Beirut and we walk to the café, bent and buried under the deliberate refusal of it, the mighty contradiction of our lives meaty weighted and unrefusing, cemented into the languorous pause of the city-state-cum-drug that is caffeine and its metaphysical apertures, wet and grinding us into dust, mercury strummed fateful resident sad but not without humor, pouring for our passage into the night, hour and full hour, in the dignity of our casual blessing, I know I must sever my life from the work we have done; this evil—and it is a white supremacist evil, among many other things, and it does not matter that it was not chiefly of my doing; I did not leave soon enough.

Even Lebanon is cursed with it—their name too means "white," and not because of the snow-capped peaks. It is because of Gobekli Tepe. Because of what we did.

"How did you know we would come here?" she says.

"We're not really here," I tell her.

"Close enough."

"Close enough for government work," and I kiss her.

Though the kiss is not enough. Falafel, not enough. The beauty of this ocean town, not enough either. Because I have been delinquent in my duties to educate myself about the consequences of my partaking of the blood of Gobekli Tepe, and donating my time to the cadences of its rapturous music.

Perhaps that is the problem, rapture, even as it is for the christians, this problem of too much of the world, too much of its pleasures, and though we can hardly deny ourselves, we are not ascetics—not yet—still we are demented in their presence, like the lotus-eaters, unable any longer to think entirely straight.

We think crooked; or at least: I do. I am a crooked thinker, as I am sure you have figured out much before I did. What you may not understand is how far crookedness can go. It can take you so far: the earth is crooked, isn't it? Crookedness is only a curve.

Curve with me, under the sun, and under my

arm, in the beneficent champignon karma and stone, with no where else to go; but by one another. Come lover under the rocks for our dinner and out into the winter summer sun; our pageantry is divine, although all this means is that it's fun. Strummed and stunned under the meadow light.

In faerie circles we will go, bent umber and amber, beckoned and burnt to know where it is we have gone.

Are we gone to love?

Are we gone to the future?

Gone under this music; I know that much. Music does not proceed in one direction alone.

I am sorry; it's true, for being crooked. Even though I know it to be necessary. And even if it weren't, it is what I am. So, although it feels funny to apologize for what I am, I must do it: it is my duty to prepare you, too, for the compromises we have already made.

18.

This winter we are sailing south. I expect we can make it as far as The Horn if we hurry. One of the children is with us. I would have taken them all. But it doesn't matter. I took Benjamin.

Goya, in his great immensity, saw in the eyes of Saturn only a demented fool. Because I am never to be as wise as Goya, I still see the Saturn cultists as evil. Or rather, as an intelligent evil. Goya's genius was to paint Saturn eating his children as a fool; and I have not come that far yet. Their propaganda still extends within me; I still find myself looking for secret, hidden reasons. Goya only showed it for what it is.

We will make it; I know. The question is what we can do on arrival.

What can I do to free the children of our realm from certain death?

But no, it is a fate worse than death. It is not their lives at stake, but their souls.

That word, soul: the spirit. They want to eat them slow.

The bait, and the augur of red; the breath, and the mental sail; heading south; into the Gulf.

The day and airway; red and charged as my hopes, not all yet dashed, waving my raft and my heart into this decision, red and slow and knowing, knowing how far it is to drop, and how dear the passage out:

19.

Lightning in yellow over the dark sky; I'm dreaming of the night I became a father, which is not yet. The future me is watching me; drinking in the purple dove-colored dark, listening to the air.

One wonders at origins but really they're already here; we are our own origin. Everything we do originates everything we are; I am the lightning.

Hum under the surface of my face; thoughts escaping like whirlpools over the oceanic courage of this woman and boy; here there is no shelter but within, over the chasm of space and the minute; etched in alabaster, gamboge and violet ash.

I make the minute south; because I am weak; and because I can see something out of the dark, some darker thing whose mane lifts my face into the bright blue of decision.

We decide in the dark, man, woman and boy; hermits and hobos; discarded refuse; Three Wise Men sans star; raft on sea.

Tell me the name of the sea and I will wish it for you; who's every sea; limitless number; enchanted direct and not any mirror; all under-keeping realms words and attached buildings—the buildings are days.

In the blue head of decision I'm building days; anarchic harbors swirling around the vortex of our bark

bark

bark

It's cold, and I hold him under my cloak, watching the rain divide the sea from the sky.

We built a temple; stretched it wide over the skull. But who ordains its mysteries and embarks over its couraged awareness of the reef and row; who makes its ebony night arrange itself so perfectly underneath our feet?

What is the nature of the relation between our bodies; and what is it I must do to sever myself from its growing weight?

The thing on the hill is my head.

20.

We arrive at Al-Khaimah and take on provisions, watching the traveler's faces for signs of recognition. I am an authorized trader for I bear our sigil but they do not know me. Probably we have five days or so before the men who are no doubt already chasing us catch up and deliver word of our escape.

The guilt is my own too; it is as though I am chasing myself.

"We must go faster," she tells me.

"We can't afford to hire anyone to row. We must make do with the wind."

"What will they do to us if they catch us?"

"I don't know. They're unlikely to kill us. They know of many fates worse than death."

I believe there is a landing site in Duqm; but if I attract one of the visitors I can't say for certain that they would help, or even understand what it is I am telling them. Likely we will have to fight before we reach there anyway.

I buy a knife from one of the sailors on the dock; its Yemeni jewel is like a dull red eye.

"Do you know how to use one of these?" I ask the boy.

He smiles.

21.

Who judges the name of men; separates its teeth from its head; its memories from its habitations; its blood from its death? Who makes the herd spur left under rock; summons wisdom for the arrival of the enemy; groks the light? Who judges the name of men; forming it watchful; locking it and marring its face, to go aground with its tumbled graces, consonants into the syllabary? Who wakes the demon of our fierce love, no nearer absence than its groan, no hereafter but its embrace? Who judges love to mean what it does? And who negotiates its absence under the creekbeds and sounds of my wakefulness, sweat dust and wind? Who judges the name of men; without their direction; without their need; hinting at their desire under the dragon of the fall; so near; and nearer; who names men under the dragon rhyming his face with the teeth; who cloaks his children and lovers in the name of the creekbed, in the skeleton of the ancestors?

Who can judge the name of men; nearer always; keeping the meaning terrible and close; bombmaker; epitaph breaker; thrower of stones?

Who judges the name of men to creep soundlessly under my head; dominating my passions; serving my will; arbitrating my body like the sea from the continent; aging the memory of our keeping for some distillation, or communicator; path through sea.

We do.

I judge the name of men an oath; rock and stone; ash and current; waking and dreaming; walking under the force of time; no never making the wind wreak, for it is we who wreak under its balcony, as the raft; nearing the hesitancy of my desire.

We can judge; winter the present under the shelter of the past until there is no more of it; and then we must move.

22.

Man and hand are the same word for our ancestors; even as the slavers measured their slaves by the hand.

Manumit and command, commando, countermand and demand, maintain, manage and maneuver; manifest, manufacture and remand, helmsman, thy manuscript is writ into your throat.

Manumit and command, helmsman, I wield your throat like a sun; strumming the boughs of the earth.

Swim with me under the deep ash earth; under the rose sun, inside the deep mother wondering after her son, the sea:

The boy is laughing, for the first time in weeks, as we swim at the shore. Already I am in love with the woman but it is no matter; what could I ever do about it?

I am only one of the pillars we cut out of rock there in Anatolia, waiting for the gods to come and occupy its face.

She is a sort of bird who will not leave; stubbornly staring through the window to see what it is I've become.

23.

we will not begin

nor win it; we have everything we wanted; it smokes and shades; it weighs and follows us a dog, bewildering

bewildering dog
unknowable dog
dog of leashes
dog of chance
and grace
dog the rumbler and the tummy stopper greeter and date
karma and place
argent and shade
the dog
we will not begin
I can't number it
can't see it
won't see it
dog
garble dog
gangly dog
message dog
mental dog
reacher dog
ambler
heavily weighted
far and aft
mercury and ace

dog
dog under and break
break even
break the air
and the name
dog of pasture and space
dog of the ready gorge
the broken lance and pace
pace in
for the keeping
we shall have no shelter here, Xenophon
but here is your dog
dog of thought
dog of hate
the lumber dog
the eager dog
of shame
come in with the dog
numberless beginning wastes
over the amber band of the bedroom
come in with the dog
for the majestic arc
for this
dog mine and weird
dog wake and rain
make halt and crane the neck to find the sound
of death
the patient quilt of the wood
the work of the temple in the dust

The dog waltzes
And I with him
Make the dog
Write the dog
Work the dog
Rank the dog
Keep the dog
Free the dog
for the dog only on the arbor's canopy
for the dog

We can discern the dog in us; waiting in the water for the will within; the ancestral call; the make and the will of the dell of the deep blue ocean blue rights blue narcoleptic corridor my own; blue and right; blue and mighty; blue and on peak; blue and unstoppable; blue and mine.

"They'll lay waste to the countryside and take prisoners; I can hear them coming."

A woman's scream.

The beat of my feet in the sand.

Sword in my hand.

I am a dog, set to action. Heeled but eager to be released.

24.

What black drum; what black face; what black reward. The graceless alleyway of the sky stands right before me. What can I do for this; who will make me. What is it I did. What black demon; stamping on my face. What terrible ordeal, menacing as the past, merchant of the devil, wrought in my teeth, making me fear myself, who will bilk the reason from my mirth, shake me to the bone, to carry me into battle?

What black demon, stemmed and defeated, menacing as the night, will keep me here, to whet my tongue for the carnal feast of blood?

What black name will I call myself, released? Demon of blood.

Ghost and god and wraith; my face; my hand to knife against the neck of some man of my own, cousin.

Cousin and cousin and lover.

"Which way did they go?"

"I don't know."

I hold it closer against his neck.

Cousin; in the family reward.

"Tell me now."

What necks will open and what decks will play whose voice; whose measure. Whose right and what charge; and will it mean anything; one boy. This one.

"He's in his tent, the master," he gasps. "Shall I

tell him you're here?"

"No," I say, and slit his throat.

Cousin, interloper mine, all my wreaths and stalks, all my killing. All of my words and deeds. All of my spite and angst; this world.

World-keeper and the melancholy rage of the deep; anchor by me; I am the dog of the sea. I will knife and fight my way to home, a place that does not yet exist.

What will it mean if I kill all the evil men; does it make me evil like them? I never ate children; but I will slit their throats in the dark, the child-eaters.

Who judges men? Who makes the world quelling over my stone heart?

Black over the Red Sea.

Barren as night; rebellious; not any man or wind; not a thing I can name. Not any reason; not the meaning.

Dog; dog to keep and marry; dog wreak and marry the world.

Dog match and war; lark and harry the door; dog catch and shake; wake to ream the marry edge; lurk and foundry rage the limpid pool of my hate; arco-rage and sundry; soundered and felling the gay fire insuperable; lamp and wick; dog.

Dog light.

This is my name; call me into the despair of night for my work.

Rake and imbue the night with my blood; hate

to kill; and then bend underneath the stone. Bend underneath the quelling stone to bake my bread, woman; over the endless fire.

There will be more. Blood on my hands I undo the ropes and push us to sea; the next party will be larger.

25.

Dog of war; my night. Barrier of the day; bilge.

I'll murder you in the night for my people. But my people no longer exist.

Let me undo the clasps of the sky; let me burn the earth.

I will not. No woman or poem. No name or wretch; no numinous face. No hatch or realm; not any language; not this life; or the next; not my name or my body but my spirit; ageless and angry; unkept wandering the dark day; give me fire for my legs; I'll walk and burn.

This angry spirit; black sand and hair; needful melody and winter; winter of loss; angle of melody and loss; we're moving in you; I won't stray; keep me under your blue sheen for just another mile.

26.

Dog make me sit; make me marry the earth. Make me dig under the earth and bury me in it; I'm bones.

I'm the bones; marry me to them; bone digger. Bone and bairn and buddy burn.

Dog me lay under the sun grown old and weary of it in my youth; no tender take or name to patient sail over the mincing heart of it, over the many counter arguments and missiles in my own mind trying to end my tale before it meets its fair end; my dog; grown and old; gained and painted fat stalwart ruminant over the barrages and takes; caught and mapped; wild for the word weird and wonderful nullifying the sack; fermenting the wrap of fate; dog under and one; meant for rocks rooks and ferries; monuments and visages; filigrees and fountains; mensch masked matched delivering the news; full year:

Dog my body; dog my run; dog my child; dare and dig my dog; dirt dust and dream my dog; diligent dark meaning mad and fame for dog; ditch and dog; alms and the sun:

It's hours in the sea. If I think I am a dog; I'm free. But I really am a dog, you see. I must be a dog. I cannot be a man.

27.

Dog for the wheat. Dog for the lamp and mendy throne under the marred ocean home; each our own underneath the burial rites; my dog; each dog; clamped and carried rough and sure through the mar and mast the milky wrath of the soundless years; my dog; no nearer than dream; no canny nor plausible ratch or mirror could dissuade it; no never further from doubt.

Dog and carry the load. I will; woman boy and the story; if it carry me too; or not too; I have the furnishing for it, my hours and manes; rocks and categories for it; the patient and the glad caught capped and named; but still no nearer; the banyan become hold; cloud and maid; ash and scars and banes; each ours; covering us in the black.

Dog. Pick up. One more hour. Ten more cycles of the watch.

Watching is nothing; compared to making.

Make dog; work dog; dog and cut; dog and curl the taste from your mouth. Dog and match the clasp and wakefulness of it; wake up.

Wake up, dog, for the year awaits; no mightier than the sun; no nearer nor farther; not any fatter; meant for you; passioned in the embrace of it; cut to order over the fat steak table; glad and minded to the whim of the majesty of the air.

What does the dog know about our sacrifices? Probably more than we. Why didn't I study with the dog at the beginning? Learn from his habits and shapes? Mean for him as he meant for me? Perhaps I did but didn't realize it.

Dog under the bench. Dog over the broad armed stare. Dog for the doom-laden and the bad; the wretched sad bewildered mad course cut fogged and dead dying pilgrims old sullen and serene; in the cut, after the freeway; nameless; burned out; still moving; the lackluster remnants of books never written; elastic; shameless and the burnt umber of our reckoning tide, brownassed and the ten o' clock rush to the stream; to see whose kingdom this is.

We are no kingdom but rage and I will harbor its voice; give me it; give me all of its names; I need every one.

We're away; nowhere at all. Each name escapes me; along with the shape of the world, coast cut and cliff; blur murk and shattered mountain; kelp over the run.

Here I can hear the glow of the world underneath my skin; incorruptible; enchanting; what sadness grows into given time; the mount of the year; the epiphany of tragedy; goat song sans goat, just man woman and child and sea; lurking divine over the cross cut chorus mad of Red Sea and sand.

28.

She is asleep. It is dangerous to look at her because then I will forget my duty. A woman is a thing; as I am; but not as I am; ridiculous. She is ridiculous; but I must not look at her.

She is a bunch of rags bundled together on my raft; one small treasure I have secreted with the boy; disaster.

No matter; it isn't for her I do it. But perhaps I am lying to myself. Perhaps it is the duty that is a lie and it was for her all along.

Perhaps both are true; and she relies on my duty so I can ignore her; as we both rely on the fiction of my loyalty and strength to bear this absurd mission to fruition.

The mission itself is like the act of love, no less absurd; some reliance on habit and emotion; the corridor of the shape of the starlit realms of the deep, churning our mass into abundance, rotund flayed and home.

Why is it then that I am the stalk, battered hasp, cloak and company parturition underneath the aggressive sky; bloodied dimple.

Rather she is a part of me; the necessary bit. I won't look.

Black battered symphony my own; arboritious; clat-ryhmed sea foam and sail:

29.

She tells me "I'm pregnant."
Abandon ship.
Just kidding.

30.
"What?"

31.

What ruinous divination charts the map of your face; hexed and scowled into reeds? Lark lake and lull, under the umber union of the soul with earth; locked hard and wrecked over the shoals of love; corded and spotted with age; rocked underneath the barley and the travails of our bounty; one thousand miles and counting, south.

What chart; what map; what ship will sail to take me there; what reason will permit me to understand its waves; capture its meaning; skirt its boundaries to my own.

"Whose is it?"

"I don't know."

What passage to beneath your words will stand to weigh the architecture of your soul; what specie or what grace will build the ace over your coal and bright barrier keep; locked loaded and sold into the treasury of the onion speakers; lake of sun; goal of carrier fire; preternatural wielder wide and deep; bay of sticks.

Claw of music; sharp steel beak; gold mercury and shame; rook of the world; what gravity can enforce my eerie mouth speaking to you; make me say the words; dram and dig their dirges and dear regards; organ of rapture.

A man is a hand; but a woman is an older thing; the word itself may mean "clit hand" or "twist hand." The specialized hand is the woman's; the man's is general.

It may also mean "shame hand."

Or "covered hand."

Cover in shame the woman from the world; or adore her openly; she does not care; she is beyond these things. We things prepare for their dissolution, and in our spirit we ready the courses for our seed; knowing their worth; measuring their distance; and agonizing over the spiral sight of their evolutions; manumissions; ordury graceful pat and fine, into the etched girth of stone water and bracken base gilt wonderment mad ocean:

32.

Not for the first time, I consider the fact that I left without any plan at all. Not that this is the worst thing in the world. But poetry does not solve every problem; nor willpower.

I mean I have a pregnant woman and a boy on a raft. And now a lot of people want us dead. This is decidedly inconvenient. What I need is allies, but all we seem to be getting is further away.

We could still go to Duqm; but relying on space aliens is just about as bad an idea as fleeing in the first place.

Not that it was a bad idea. It just seems I wasn't entirely prepared for it. You leave behind the blood, but it keeps following you.

What does it mean to leave it behind? When you have to keep doing things? I know my mind is diseased; but it is this quality precisely which gives me a chance to defeat the cabal.

33.

We're off to see the aliens, because we want to see just what it is they've done. Just who are these aliens. Just how did they become so alien. And why is it they insist on hovering around in the sky?

Are they dancing? What are they singing?

Can you dance to it? Are they beneficent? Magnificent? Will they heal the pain in my heart?

Can I get them to attack a city for me?

What is that special shape they make in the air? And that special sound? And that special feeling in my head, when they're coming down?

What will happen if I touch one of them? Are they just like me?

How far away are they? And how close?

Will they really know what to do? Do I really know what to do?

How did I get here, asking ridiculous questions like this?

34.

There's almost nothing I know; I am this burnt wisp of a leaf; scattered through the sun, and squinting to see the horizon:

To be delivered. Whose burden is the past; the link under sky to my birthplace, watching me behind my back?

Each man subsists himself in the insistence that there shall be no more; I've written it out, the circumlocutor is done and I will have my vengeance, or only my word, to cut it short, and say;

Now.

Now.

In the primordial soup of everyday life, these ambulators will have no regard for us; do not come closer.

Each man decides where he will stop.

But conversely, in leaving, the birthplace and the birthpeople object similarly: we can not in good conscience permit you to leave, because you are part of us.

I take the weed and garment; the hum under word; elision of the encoding; syllable for syllable, ribonucleic:

Still mine. Or mine again. And south.

I will not winter with you.

In the great hierarchy of being, who decides what is permitted?

I am my own god; only I can decide.

It is not permitted.

Scuff and weight; my body the driest hasp under wing; lesion:

Wear me under the path out and I will be weary for you;

Still exact, and melancholy. In my disaster I've found release, and friends.

And if I find enough, I will come for you.

- -

Bear me south; for I have seen things in the sky; our friends.

35.

We've camped in a wood by the sea.

"Where are we going, master?" the boy asks.

"A place where I hope we can find friends."

"The alien friends?"

"Yes."

"Will we fly in their ship?"

"I don't know. I would advise against it."

"I hope we can."

"Are you ready to go?"

"Yes."

- -

I push us out into the water and climb back aboard. Each new realm we encounter—sea to air; air to space—forces us to change. Sometimes I wonder whether the people from the sky are not ourselves, returned and changed.

Or perhaps it is that we are the changed ones, returned from there. As the whales and dolphins returned to the sea.

There is little wind and so I row along the coast, watching the brown-yellow shape of it disappear into itself, and the sea, as we move.

"Peace" means "covenant" and so it must be that the peace of the sea is its covenant with the earth and sky, and us with it. A system of agreements along the water's edge.

There is too much darkness behind me; I don't even want to think about it. Or what I can do about it. Perhaps my hope in our friends in the sky is simply an aspect of my own powerlessness. Surely it can be nothing else. Maybe it's possible that my sheer folly in leaving so soon and unprepared will jar them into helping us. If not, perhaps we can stay aboard this little boat forever, and I will raise the boy and the unborn child of this woman as my own. I would like that.

She's wretching over the side.

"Is she all right?"

I look back and see the ship. Just the edge of its mast at the horizon. I'm damned, I know it. All I can do is row faster.

36.

No one will see me; not if I row fast enough. Not if I hold fast to the day into the night. Not if these things I see, which look like the demands of an angry god, sent to terrify and destroy me, can dissolve into the light and dark, shapes of my own mind, succored inside.

No one will see me; not yet. Not until I have prepared for them my vision; built the thing who will destroy them.

The devil in me knows they're friends; that I am not so different. That if I took two steps to right or left I could be like them, make like them, live and die with them. But the steps are farther than they look. These tiny differences: like my tiny oars, set against the great sea.

I can see their ship getting larger; but the day is growing long. It will be a moonless night.

I set my burning shoulders into the water, stubborn deliverer, bent wizard fresh out of his spells, but still with his hat, to cover his head.

No one will see me until I open my eyes; not that part I keep away, in waiting. Listening to the dark to shield my inner night against the day; whose righteousness is also deceiving, since light does not care what happens in it. Rather it is the recording device, temperamental but persistent, keeping watch over the map and weight of our deeds, so as to know what to do next.

I watch the water under my hands; growing black; purple and black. As wine is dark so are my shoulders, bent under the task, to build myself a new world.

"What is it they want?"

"To eat us, in the name of their god."

"Why do they want to do that?"

"They're mad."

"What are we going to do?"

"Shhhh."

The water is turning from blue to red in the light; and from red to black. Striated frames of the night, the water and the light; somehow I know what it is I will do, but cannot put it into words; it must be I am already doing it. What this thing is, my body over the water, and this boy, but also the sound it makes, in the mind and in the air, of our beings set against the waves, to victory.

The rose of victory is not on this earth; but in the sky. I can see it wavering there, under the sun, swept over the shape of the horizon the great sheet of the world, flapping over our warm bodies struggling to escape all the demons who call us their friend.

37.

I can feel her arm over my body and for a moment I don't remember if we made it to shore or are still afloat; then I hear the sound of the water but realize I am not moving with it. The tiniest of inlets cut into the brown earth is our night in the dark.

I can't really feel my arms but they still move when I tell them to, pushing my body up off the ground to look into the night.

How near she is, and so fragile, the night, like a woman. It feels as though one sound could make her go away. Though she is also eternal.

There is some life in my body; it's waiting for its orders, but its orders are "wait" and it doesn't like that.

I remember who I was; but only for a little while longer now. Soon those doors will be shut for good; I welcome that.

Soon they'll take me out and thrust me into the world; more glorious than it ever was.

How frightening is this world, the near lady, now reprehensible, but stone, marked into denudement prescient and scraped into the water:

Part of me is unsure now if I am on the water or on the earth, although I know I am on the earth.

What can a killer do to killers? I suppose that's all it is. One shade of denudement of matter, whose earth rides over my back, illustrious.

I fit the knife into his chest, and over the other's head I fit the bag, to turn him down into the water.

I take his bow and sight the main sail; almost eight feet tall. Too far to fire.

What I must do it something beyond me; fight empire with empire. Kings by becoming king. What an absurdity. Ing ing ing all the live long day.

"Into the desert."

This is what the word Arab means; desert. I walk behind my boy and woman. I turn to look: our little boat is another of the corpses.

Each black agent and fire; sure and speedy, named wrought handed and lanced; the liquid fire of the world, for some minutes in my name, this is what I must find in the Horn.

Really the liberation of slaves cannot be done swiftly, you see. I wish that it could. But there are too many things in the way. Still, that is for later. Cutting their bonds is the fast part.

- -

I know that I am already dead; that this narrative reaches you from my afterlife into your own. I who worshiped death have been made sane by it; here, there are no more worries.

Perhaps this is also a lie; is it not my urgent worries which bring my words to you, some angry ghost?

38.

Somali means go and milk.

Who blesses us in the night? Us guests known for our wanderings; never far from fear, lifted into the buckets of these pastoralists, carrying our danger like the ashes of an ancestor, tight to our chest.

I haven't any money but they don't seem to need it; requiring of us only that we tell them our story.

"In a last ditch effort to conceal what I knew from my masters, I asked to be put on assignment, to rove the countryside and interview witnesses about some thefts which had occurred from our farms."

The old man watched us carefully, smiling faintly, clutching his walking stick, as I spoke.

"I soon realized I would have to join the thieves if I discovered them; while I still felt loyalty to my tribe to my leaders I did not. They are become monsters and so I have pledged to destroy them, though this will likely mean my death. The woman comes with me because she also desires my death, though not by their hand but by hers."

The old man smiled at this and offered us his pipe, which we took. Out of the fragrant night the music of the forest swept over us like a dark bird, shielding us from the light.

39.

I cannot say who it is I've become; likely it doesn't really matter. I have said enough, to my masters, and to my people, and now what I've said will grow into my future.

I can detect some wavelength from the stars; moving over my head like a woman, bent under her washing, bent over me, riddling the night. It may be I am undone entirely, and that these memories of mine are false, eidolons from some previous era, which I pretend to know. Of course one must live as though all one experiences is real; to do otherwise is madness. But I have never been as good at knowing which parts to ignore.

We are dancing around the fire with the Somalis. Some of them object to my light skin, and inquire if I am quite well. I tell them honestly that I am not, and this seems to satisfy them. The drums go on all night. They are summoning something here; I hope it is something which will help us.

When we examine the problem we can detect that those things which have meaning adhere to the body like blossoms in air; seeds stuck to the skin. The meanings grow and change one, mutating the course of one's life. It has been so with me but probably this is a commonplace.

"Have you seen men like me on the sea?"

"Yes, some."

"How recently?"

"Three nights past."

"They may be back. Did they say anything?"

"We traded fish with them."

"Did they ask about me?"

He shook his head.

- -

I lay next to the boy on his bed of leaves.

"Are you all right?" I asked him.

"Are you all right?" he asked.

"Yes. I've spoken to the chief and we are welcome to stay as long as we like. But probably we will have to move on in a few days, if you're ready to travel."

"The men who are hunting us, are they here?"

His voice sounds like reeds in the wind.

"No, they're not here. But they will be."

"Will the chief help us?"

"He might. But he might just as easily turn us over to them if we demand too much. We should tread lightly."

"I'm tired," he said.

Overhead are small meteors; flickering over the stars.

"Look, do you see?"

I can see his eyes, wide and aglow. But he says nothing.

40.

We can decide certain things and not others; if I am a creature of the stars it is not through any will of my own; not any decision of mine. Some people claim all things are influenced by them; that we are their slaves. I do not say this but rather that I was taken prisoner by them in middle age; perhaps part of this story is my effort to free myself from them.

I lay on the grass to try to remember my origin—that is, the simple fact of remembering where I was born, where I grew up, what it was like. I find it more and more difficult to remember. I know this is a common enough occurrence, but for me it takes on a dangerous air, slipping into the night side of my life, from where I fear I will not return:

In the shade I bark, a dog. Entering into the night time, with its many doors.

Who will I meet? Who will I be? What will I say to them? I am standing, under the dark night, and its sky, feeling the damp air on my skin. Somewhere near the woman is sleeping; or pretending to sleep. She is the only thing keeping me here now; not even the boy, which is a terrible thing to say. If I were a better or more honorable man . . .

Still, I have promised to save him. What kind of man am I if I can not even do that?

The stars are dancing over my head, and I with them. I move through the grass, half naked, jumping a bear into my den, not in the stone but in the sky:

Who is it with me; and what is it; the name of my being, not words but a feeling: the direction of my life.

Who is it named me, not my mother, or my relatives. Not me either. Not even these stars. Who wrote the names in my book, writing them over my eyes, into my hands, to make me dance:

There are doors in the night; whose face is neither day nor dark but light: in his reaches I have been marking time, to know what it is I do on this earth, to try and understand the feeling in my head, that all things which have order come from far away, as light itself, from distant suns. We are the direction finders, dogs listening for the sound of the memory, or future memory, of meaning:

"Come we have to go," I tell the boy. He wipes the sleep from his eyes. The woman sits up from her bed beside him.

"Are you coming?" I ask her.

We're going; but I have never felt more incompetent as guide. Perhaps it is better to be sacrificed into the wilderness than to live as a slave; but I am not always certain of that.

41.

We're leaving, and I'm singing the song the ancestors gave me, about music, and what it is. Who made music, and what for, and in what light, and what form, should you invite the storm to come and take hold, take hold of us in its fell curtains, to accord us its night; I have the whiskey with me but I'll give them none; so I can be ready for what it does.

We're counting corridors; we're mad. Mad in the desert sea.

I won't tell you anything but me; what I did. They did other things but it wasn't me. I don't know what they did. I only barely know what I saw; who I was, then, moving away from Somalia, away from Potbelly Hill, out into the light.

This song is about memory, and what it does; and whose turn it is, to tell you, how we were made. Which cut and which scamp shall break the seal over the message in the air; riddles and poems; and the augury in the simple spark of light over your hand; meditating on your right to see:

See us here, under the sound, daggerlight and fall to speak, which wound and which hand, shall I break; shall I brand with my name:

Each name in its sequence, never muttered slow nor hurried but in time; ready for mark

mark seventeen

eighteen

nineteen

The music starts under my ears; inside my shoulders; and who will insist; who will know; who will blame or accord us the names we've been searching for; the name of the not-king; and the name of the not-queen, a thing we can know only through the imagination; as it's never been seen.

Maybe the king is right; this imaginary king who does not exist; maybe he is right that he is the land; because the land just barely exists anyway; is merely this tendency to be, under certain conditions which keep changing, and so the land has to decide, just like the king, who he's going to be. Who he's going to name, and how much he wants it to matter.

"We're going to drown in this rain," she says.

"I'm sorry. I wasn't thinking."

"We can take shelter in that wood."

"Yes. Lead the way."

The name of the music is something I can't hear; but I can see it in the boy's face.

- -

Now I won't remember anything; the darkness comes over me like a cloak; I'll forget names and faces and the words of my language; the reason I am alive. Now in the silence of the storm I can be free, or something close to it—a word I fear no longer exists, or never did.

This is all right; we suppose that memory is necessary but really it is only an additional accoutrement, a sort of vestigial organ which does no harm but is not necessary for life.

Memory is as easily ordered as the rest of your life, in that you can order it any way you like; or do away with it if this is your will.

Of course I am afraid to enter the present moment; but it is the fear which motivates me. What lies inside it and the earth and the trunks of the trees and the sounds of the woman's voice, stroking the boy's hair.

What marches our ideation into the glistening reality of our bequeathement, into and out, in rhythm, breathing: breathing not with our lungs but our brains, in and out.

If you cover the idea in your mind, hide it just enough, under your jacket, and let it peek out, like a squirrel into the dark, with small dark beady eyes, ready to judge the world without a sound, and know its reflexes, out of your ordered bliss and silence.

We're sheltered under the canopy; and though I am mad—anyone will tell you this—I fear I have discovered the path we are meant to walk. Into the dark:

Cover the idea in your mind for the universe is hungry and will wish to eat it; do not let it know what you intend. Be brave, and hide: and in hiding conquer.

42.

No aspect of togetherness shall be inscribed for I am immune; or rather every aspect of it shall be: I am not really writing this.

We like to toss around these ideas, like that you are me and I am you. As though it is amusing dinner conversation. Quite otherwise when we explore it; the absoluteness of it. No one may order it otherwise; memory has no hold over it, nor can Man separate himself from the reality of the idea; from all realities.

I would not intend to separate you from anything; I have no power at all. I have only been here for a time wondering, and will soon go; and I will tell you some of the things I have seen.

This woman wears yellow, and has a small boy. She has dark eyes, like mine. The eyes of the woman tell me we are in danger, and that this excites her. The boy is afraid and I can see his eyes too, needy and wide. Overhead the trees are speaking to us in their language, and I am not able to not listen; their voice is like the woman's eyes, unconquerable. The light of the ocean over her face.

Of course it is for her I left; I see that now—or rather I am blind to it, because I need to be. I can hear the sound of the owl, who is the eternal present. And the sound of the mouse, huddling close to us, watching for crumbs.

The boy is eating a piece of cheese, pressing it

hard against his face, under the rain.

My own hand looks like an alien's—some other man, or being's. This is how it is supposed to be. How terrible it would be for me to know myself—it would be an awful surrender.

The boy hands a piece of the cheese to the woman and she eats it too, glancing at me and the sky, waiting for the rain to stop.

I'm going to open my mouth and speak: words will come out of my mouth to inform my companions about something of the nature of this journey, but these words will be ridiculous and so I will soon stop speaking. What the story is is not ours; nor can I describe it, or give any name to it or reason; it is far better to say nothing at all about it. In this fashion I can preserve its essence for the time it takes to be over. It will be over; I know it: it's how it is, these simple things. But it is also necessary for me to deny these simplicities, to make them as complicated as possible, to bring the meaning out, even if it is only private, only mine, something I can carry away deeper than memory, like a scar, or a road, a wave of light over the sky and the mind.

The moon is peeking out between the rainlit leaves and we are all looking at it. We are wondering when the rain will end, and when our lives will start.

"I love you," I say, but it is to neither the woman nor the boy, nor even both, but to the nature of our being in the forest, and what it meant to be there when I was a man in Africa.

43.

I am dreaming; but I am awake, as I feel you may know. Please don't think ill of me; it was something I had to do. The same way you might have to have dinner with a friend—even a friend you no longer even like. Or the way you must look at the sky, even though you've already looked at it four or five times, just in the last thirty seconds.

Ordination is what I am after; this is a kind of grief. Ordination is like coordinates: it is to be called Coordinate-Maker.

In the stomach of grief, we can be sound:

Love me in the dark no feeling nor pressure: no sound.

I will grow closer to the love of life, even as I fear where I am going, who I'm becoming, the world I've made. Take me and be afraid, for I am lonely, and this is my story: unending, and without reason, meant for a storm, who has already arrived, and in its leaving I will be even more dead; closer to death than ever before, its manservant, its computer, ordinateur, coordinate system for the interlocking plates of the cosmos, mesmerically arranged for our play.

On our left, we have god, and on our right, a woman, and I in the middle will play referee.

god- I don't want anything to do with this.

woman- Just what do you think you're doing?

me- Illegal move: posturing.

god- this won't get any better.

woman- you could at least have brought us more to eat.

god- she loves you: don't you know that?

me- what is love, god?

god- nothing, or a sort of nothing. Nothing at all.

woman- he's right.

me- if it's nothing, then why do you care so much about it?

god- well why do you care?

me- I want to know, I want to know just what it is. Won't you tell me.

god- You have to figure it out for yourself. I already told you that. Get some sleep, why don't you.

woman- I'm lonely.

me- I know.

woman- won't you love me?

me- I'm trying.

god- there, you see? It's not that hard. Just shut up for a minute and do your job like a good boy. I'm watching you.

me- Shut up god, you're always watching us and you never do anything. Fuck.

god – I'm sorry.

me- Illegal moves: no apologies.

woman- Are you boys done whipping out your dicks? There's work to do.

44.

I don't know what work is, even though I do it. What is work?

What is the knowledge we gain from doing?

What are we doing?

We're going, never to return. But what is the doing of it? What is it to do something? These acts of creation, the terrifying presence of your body made to move and act and mark the world with your desire.

"Where are we going?" she asks me.

"South."

But it could be any direction.

We're not moving, though we're walking. It would be my life to move; to leave; revenge, or something like it: escape, my old dream.

Although such things are impossible it doesn't make them any less attractive—probably more so.

I'll bury you at midnight, when we're gone, and the ships have sailed and the sun has set, and I have no feelings yet. When death comes for me and I have done my bit for the scars and ruins, writing them over the corpse of beauty we wrought.

No light may flame the dark, for it is with us as we step through the wood, independent of any movement of the sun, moon or stars. The dark is something we carry inside, the heavy fluid of being, meant to order and relate the world into our hands, bending us into it, like now, as I walk, watching the rain.

Work with me in inaction, set to stun the ruins into light, not from any source but in the trickle of our thoughts down into our feet, gestating mushrooms; plants; seasons and events, like your walk with me, and the boy's.

There is no shelter within; storm of rock in solitude of thought; light and breath benumb the ordination of our presences and doubts to form the wind and rain; engulfing the mystery of our destinations within these days and nights, enraptured:

I will make the city without rooves to make our name important, blasted and fair, the rook in the kingdom I see staring us down at the edge of an interior wood: happy portal.

Where are we going, so near, meant to recover some prize, memory, or puzzle, the saint's regard and slavery in our nights: excellent and dearer than sleep, the elocution of a city-world who is like your own heart, invisible.

Where are we going, foundered and mad, but still with cheese. We still have some left.

45.

And if I could stop, what would it mean to do it? Stop what? This; this thing; what I've come in to possession of. Here we are; each body, reluctant to take hold of, full of fear, but the quiet fear, of nearness, relatedness, and the distance that is in nearness and relatedness. And out of that, exhaustion.

Leave that?

The Biblical characters (men who have yet to come into existence) always know what to do; their god tells them, or their Bible (of course), and so seized with their certainty (and the improbable and immediate support of their people), they slay and drive out the interlopers, the baby eaters, the unclean and unholy self-eaters who thought to rule their kingdom.

It works so well in the Bible.

The Bible comes from Byblos, which only means mountain. Yet another god, unknowable and slow, made out of stone, wind and rain.

Here we are, in the Bible, of stone wind and rain, run amok, and grinning at each other in our unlikely postures. Threatened with death and overjoyed.

I kiss her in the rain. It is like a seal, whose meaning cannot be written.

Each man must do the work, unholy too itself, written alone, unbothered, direct or indirect, the blasted arc of a dead sun, but revivified through the transmigrations of time into your present moment, never nearer, the awesome breadth of your own devotion to it, reality bequeathed to you by large cousins, bodies in space.

I kiss her but it isn't enough; who was it said that the earth was enough? All of these things. That it should be such a burden is enough, not caught by far, not countable, not surmisable, or broken, not the thing itself but the phantasm, my phantasm, come closer won't you, so I can tell you all my secrets, when I was a man on earth.

When I was a man on earth, I dreamt great things, without rhythm or chords, blasted stack of meat, ornery bacon and marsh, wrought willed dressed and stuck in the dark, mad and triumphant:

When I was a man I dreamt of you; never nearer, not worldly, not enough: not this again, and not my own, not hearing, or sight, not the meaning, or the door, but the passage through:

Work and man fill me with this tight stomach and cramped back; turning over myself, to look:

We're going;

Going;

Black with me, under the night, bear and hide, hood and raft of feet, in the mud. The dark angels of the past in the sky keep us warm in the rain, we have no need of our words; for they are all around us, plummeting us into the fall:

Who would say they had me; looked at me; knew me; but I knew her.

Bear with me the mud, and the frightened rain, and the ardor of the gasp in twilight under our tarp, watching the sky light up. The cheese is warm and stinky and the night fires are warm in our breasts, not Anatolia but Africa, not Africa but the silence of morning; arched and rotted, like an old tree, grinning down at me through the years and laughing.

I knew her when I was young and now am old, but the time moves in both directions; for I can touch his lips too, and tell him who I will be, when I am young again:

Never enough; for if I would fight with you I would fight with everyone, and say no to this world; I will have a better one.

In my boots and back. In my eyes and hair. Hovering over the sky.

"They're coming down!" She's shouting.

They take us into their craft and away, out of the storm, and out of the life I had known.

But this journey is only one part of it; the other part runs underneath, demanding like Proust to know just what has occurred, and who is in charge here.

I demand to see the manager and have a full accounting, and you're it, and I would have you write down every expense, every penny and kopek, to know just who it is you've become, and who you were, and who you will become again, when you have met yourself over this road, never passing, never pausing, but gazing forever over your shoulder, watching the road succeed and decline, yourself:

I knew you better than I knew me although that is hardly a compliment. And if we're leaving it's because of you. I'm sorry that I couldn't do more.

And if there is something alien it is in myself, not the UFOs. But you already knew that.

Inside the black raft of memory I want you to know what's important: it wasn't me who was there but it was you. And I want you to tell me everything you remember. What you saw and who you met. What you said isn't important; you won't remember anyway. I want you to remember what it was like there, and tell us, so we can check our records, and see if it makes sense.

Have you been there, in space? And whose beauty was it, cut around your shoulders, like a bear's? And was I with you? I want so much to be.

Part 2

46.

We're gone; and I'm sorry about that. I'm sorry I ever came here, or thought to stay.

When you go someplace, it's not true, that you're still you. Not quite. Not quite again:

We're sitting in a room, but it's not a room, and it's not us. And this is what we said:

(But first let me say: to present the unpresentable or translate the untranslatable we are presented with two options: one, apply metaphor to approximate (though this too is the wrong word, for the most part) something of the circumstances beyond the ken of our language, or, two, say nothing whatsoever. While this second option may well be the better one, I have chosen the first.)

Probably I should begin with light rather than dialogue. How often we overlook how strange light is to begin with, how determinant of the full range of values of our expressions, and how odd a property of the cosmos it is when examined. It cannot surprise us that Isaac Newton took so long to come about; light is very strange, and we are much happier when we ignore it.

We know, for instance, that light attaches to itself the property of the object from which it emerges, sending in all available directions that information about its original body. But there is no original body: only a series of intermediaries.

So too, my journey with our friends can be understood, however partially, as one set of cosmic events set in a series of intermediaries. As light flickers over gravitational lenses, bounces off intervening meteoroids and starlets, or swallowed by the occasional black hole, so too my time with them was this interstitial creation of the universe, something with a time limit, but no discernible origin or culmination. In this, we might say my journey was still at least partially allegiant to Aristotle: it had a beginning and an end, though neither was ultimate, and it took place, for the most part, in one place. Whether our journey with them also had unity of theme is something only you can decide; I am too close to it to offer an opinion.

I have heard no scientific thesis regarding the relationship between photons and quarks, the latter particle something we now know is able to make decisions, and vote as groups, on how to instantiate themselves in this universe. Whether photons, being presumably equally "conscious" in some way, also exhibit this voting behavior I cannot say. But I do know that my experience of that journey was marked with a series of feedback loops, not unlike certain kinds of dreams, or for that matter even hours spent on the highly observable and intermediated social media of the early 21st century, where what one prefers to see and what one does have a discernible and measurable correlation.

Perhaps all of this is beside the point; but in any case what I wanted to begin with was the experience of light itself: how we feel when we are perceiving light.

Already to me it seems to have a duality: that it is both something from which we feel we must hide, and something to which we are drawn inexorably. Like death, in that sense. The ultimate gravitor. Light obviously carries with it this sense of wonder: we can and do experience its expression as a thing of great beauty, and it shows us both distant galaxies and nearby plants and animals in indescribable detail, when Nature so chooses to cooperate.

Probably this final sense is that which should dominate this portion of my narrative, however far I am able to make it go: whatever is tellable of it is that which Nature chose to make so. Sometimes she does the translation for me.

We were invited into their craft, and found ourselves some time later imbued with the movement of light over our faces.

Where on Earth, or in near orbit, light on your face means as you know that we see things—that light delivers to us that information about its intermediating bodies—onboard their ship we seemed to see only the light itself, some other layer of information it contains which is usually concealed.

And within the light were stories.

47.

In Unity I was a Keeper for many years until I became a Canyon, for reasons I still don't understand. Each light force from the kingdom of my ancestors moved me into places I would rather not dwell on, simply because they occurred in a place which was not my own; and can never be.

Each vibrato over the surface of my distinction—peak to peak—should be understood as a kind of string stretched through my body, beginning in space and ending there, and passing in the interim through the depths of the mountain passage of which I was a part.

In Keeping one can maintain the illusion of power but not as Canyon; but while it's tempting to think that one is the material in the first and the receptacle in the second you're really a receptacle in both; even as jokers can say truthfully that the human body is properly regarded as a toroid; hollow from mouth to anus.

I slipped into stone; whose heart I made my own; and what worth it was still stamps my mind in a beautiful lesion, scar of the past light, imprinted into my body's memory like temple candles, a thousand tiny stars, these generations keeping my thoughts down low under the table, to tremble in the divinity of this strange and shifting spirit, now so numb that I cannot properly speak; still, I bring what I can to you, Guest, to name you if I can, brother.

The mountain watches too; my love; we're waiting for you to understand.

48.

Underneath and sun; her heart.

I won't pause nor patch in this call; who heard it last. Triumphant. Under my cousin I should be regarded as vast but will not be. Think of me small: river. Little pinochle staff and shruck, stern and struck to weigh the bitterness of our cull, pressure and weight:

Too late.

Not too late for love but too late for the sun, whose ocean we encompass, as Thales worshiped us so too do we worship it, our occasional interlocutor, bright dart and drink to becalm us winter and spite, mere loveliness.

In delivering only the modicum of weight to bear on this our spirit, the shadow of a gram, hear my kingdom lamplight murmur her edges to you, drifter; in the licking of your soul I shall be revived:

49.

And air;
Never lovely, nor gone, not yet.
Who strange my music sheer and stained starting mad shall bite and beg my moon and raft to sound the harm; my harm is this:
I cannot speak but through others.

50.

I'll speak for air; I'm light.

I hinge his weight and fair into over fairings, bilking the nourishment of his need to spare words dances and heirlooms into his grasp, not any measure of it, but to say who we have been.

I bore his need for a great long time. And what I could tell of it I will not; but what I can't tell you is this: I loved every minute of it. It was something I needed to do.

51.

I too speak for air; I'm only dirt; wrinkled and mad. Come drink in me and be well; I have seen him hovering here, a mere child, delighted to see me spill his armaments over my eaves; lore that sparks rhymes a hundred miles high.

52.

Each of my children are also my fathers; mountain.

He who drinks from my gully listens to my well; now the memory of my past. She who has been riven over my weight masses the umber urgency of my throne; not stone but fire.

I have been him in time; I'll be him again. Now knocking on my horn; spiral sad and wintery, the beckon honey; pasture all-light, walked around and in the dark; his lilt describes the patterns in my ribs, dark, and ribboned with the loaves of my skin.

My words won't record; I have been speaking too long. Go awhile under my dress, I have been holding the place so you can sleep; each hour rests my hands for your work in the dark, of dreams, so I may know who it is that I become:

53.

He'll eat my salad, and my rain, he'll park my alleyway up yours; birch and seed and stamen and sand; hear me; I who am merely the surveyor of these wild lands; not pharaoh nor the ringlets he wore; not his wife nor their many children; nor Africa, nor Uranus, but the limpet stare and shirkle, mad hot and bleeding; Park Avenue mad; mad not only in the dining room but in the ovary; in the philosophy even, and the philosophers' beard, and beer belly;

I wish I had less patience for myself; that I would get old, or weary; I wish I had age like my ancestors; and like my children; I wish so many things but I am nameless in the urgency who gives shape to my need; fire

The bullet and rain; the train and shuffle stone; my work.

This is my work and you don't need to hear it; you are it, in every working cymbal section of your little cells, striated and starving, winter-mad, the deeds of years, wrapped up in a moment, of my thought:

54.

We're patient, folding in, coruscadant shuffle and mordant ember touching your skin: leaning in: boasting:

We're so far away—so close—your brother.

The stars in the land are your stars; inexorable unexitable passionkept mountain humming the bairn wee and bright-eyed, burial rite sky:

Heed our burial rite sky; no other place for it; not anyone else's business; not these words nor those but your own.

Page and bear the ankle-deep red and rain; my love. Oak and rest your need; never here, but close: the battle and bane for your love; exact underpinning sad and main:

We'll wield it and arc your shorn and scattered god into the deep; how else could we take it?

How else for you. Limpid and entire; the full mat of the iron.

We do not shine; we wrinkle. We do not twinkle; we endear induce and thrill the scar and skate bull and bend to bomb your weight under the mast:

Hold us on; we'll give you some words if you like. You can keep them in your pocket. Never nearer never gone never exact as our eyes are; our words must move three places at once; to protect you.

Hover us down a way under your feet; we're sleeping there, your stars, a damp blanket for you to keep walking.

Entire and exact, our bodies graceful sad shaking our birds and bees; our knees; we wait for you, embarker; thee.

How else would free or fail to burn us in our need; awk and keel and vest; the nimbus of our tongue.

Tell us: what do you think you'll do?

55.

Lightning over my shoulder; it makes me tremble in my mouth. My eyes blink awake. I'm a mountain; I know that. I know who I am in the dark.

The fear fields the weight; magnets and acid. Black hues and news of the force singleting my arms and hands; each many servants of my staid girth and shaker spiral dam; heat and brake; gentry and freemen meditating composure for the great push out:

The storm covers my eyes with white.

56.

"Robert are you there?"

I hold on to her hand.

"What is it?"

It's some kind of investigation of the self. But I can't say it aloud.

"Robert?"

I squeeze her hand again.

"I can't see you!"

I hold on to her tight; and over our heads the pack of metal darts shifts into second:

57.

Who heeds and hears the meant and reel, my love, short ordered and scaled to time and being; maker murderer and height. Wapt waked and run; apple dairy funnel skirt and sun: broadbacked and summoning the world:

Who heels and bakes the mansioned fears and welts for each our mercury appeals, my love, the pealing ants and shadows shaking our round mast; ineluctable but also easily escaped; hold on:

We're the nutty butter; awkward stunner shameful mad and simmering the youth for our work:

Black and new.

Who heard the sound of our dart; only yarn. Spinning around the barn to lead the child home.

Kid, are you coming? Dinner's almost ready.

Each pink sunset ocean in our beginning; liquor and skin. Shimmer and sin, my love, our bake resonates the moon—and all moons—to our vapor back and pull; auburn drool marzipan tight; embered bread closing the naked dusk.

We're here at the point of departure; leaving; leaving; lurid and leaving; loved:

Bayonet my heart; brake and steer:

No steed may race us here; we are light.

58.

Twinkle twinkle little star we'll hose the deep; arms rans and keeps; mael and shandy strum and stone my home; alone we fire our breast; augury's rest: the red and the botched clad kid; dark and beloved kid; racing around the dark.

Twinkle twinkle little star my only one; epaulette and curl; race and fulment over the sad mass of Man; an agent with a will, embarking:

How my sunder shirks the fence; my fundaments adhere like brittle ice; how my wonderment appears exact but it's spilling round the passageway with our batteries;

How I mutter what you are.

Twinkle twinkle little bartlet; plump and scad; rocked rolled and mad; auburn and heady shot out from our body; cut off:

wrinkled and meant for the deep drop down and pull back:

Our celebration out from the world.

Here we'll night the king and queen; night the day; night the pageantry and screen; night the meadow and the scene for our departure from these realms, my love; no never nearer; not a bonny dip but a full lustrous pull into the scarified embarments here abouts; augmented shrouded fell and graced; the faces of the moons and the moons of faces bordering our grizzled fires bemused and ready to fire;

Fire, my love. Shroud your hair with the music of this fuel.

Shakespeare thought the cormorant fed its young on its own blood; do that; be cormorant for us in this instant; shake your bosom and bond the burial weight of the now to our star chart; locked and culled and wet and shredded for the fire:

We see the green light; like marsh, wrinkled over the vast black:

Pistons and sounds of the port.

Faxflax endow the reef and bear; we're ready.

"Prepare the weights."

Some sound.

"Hold on to your hats."

Fire overhead.

"We're coming about."

Hissing.

"Count to five."

Red.

"Four."

Blue.

"Three."

Yellow.

"Two."

Black.

"One."

The musical and the city; some captured weight of it . . .

"Here we go—"

59.

Black and chapter weighty redded threaded to mark the hardship channel suffix of it; mercury sped throats.

"Hmm."

Captain captain who makes us here without; who is it shouting; I hear his voice.

"We've got a storm coming in fast; bear your weight low; here we go!"

Ock and bow; sallow ho; stare stilt and sun:

Electric fire

"Who is broadcasting on this channel?"

Mire and waste

"Coming about!"

Fire and fender fate—

"Disconnect: now!"

60.

Red

"We've been here before."

Red and red.

No canyon keep; no carrier; no compulsion; and no error:

"Simmer down; we're closer now."

Big breaker mad.

"This is ten four; barrier reef seventeen, carrier wave alpha ten mark ampersand Hugo. We've got ten to go; countdown begins in ten minutes. We've been here before; wave to your shadow, kids! Take a picture for your book."

The light and love are shining outside my window . . .

"Hold on to your seats; we have some entertainment for our riders who would like it; and there's guided meditation on deck two; otherwise just relax and visualize the names of your ancestors.

"Read your book . . . we're coming in closer."

61.

We bind the self to matter but its boundary is not one body, but many. In this language cooperates, as places like Sweden and *the self* come from the same Indo-European **s(w)e* root; self and group, the same.

Similarly, the group is never fixed, as you know. It shifts. It moves. New people arrive.

Out of the sky aliens appear; and in darkness names are written into aether, and from their sterling arms and hands, arbitrated through the galactic fluid, we make friends.

Lovers and arbor dwelt.

Make new the root under the dew; whose herd and welt showed firm and felt the new: each avenue is true for you, my dear, if you want it.

"We're lowering into the pit."

I hold on to the pole like a subway rider; bent under the need of the thing.

What is the boundary?

At every scale of matter in your body. At the door to the self; ageless and unheeded; mirrored plastic and bitter skunk and thrill; the black murk tails to whip you into smarts. Whose pageant. What rook.

So it is a mistake to see the traveler as one thing, nor the countries through which he travels. Each footstep parturates the self and body. Shifting from second into third:

Who heard our music and comes in to hear? Who blesses the night with his huge face, alabaster soot and wealed red mane, country neighbor.

Country neighbor from beneath the sky, beneath the ageless things we call the world, wreak with us the bed and boundary crossers in our souls, incorruptible.

Unbreakable vast. Make us chief over this shirked soiled cul de sac for an hour; we'll terrorize it, entomb it, take and bury and whirl it, write over its face our names.

"Count down to the descent."

Black names and faces.

"Five."

Arms and legs.

"Four."

The sound of the galley slave, rowing.

"Three."

His face, bent in earnest hatred.

"Two."

The waters beneath, green and black.

"One. We're descending."

All the darkness of the world hovers over my face; I can no longer feel the pole.

62.

White and coral grey and blue; colors like a tomb. My body is shaking. I can't feel the woman and boy anywhere nearby. It's better to forget: that's part of what this journey is. Making room for a new self. A new history.

63.

Green for a thousand miles. An ocean of green; the color of an inquisitive insect, unabated, shimmering green.

I see it both with my eyes and the ship's; settling down, and sliding in.

The wind is the sea's; some sea I've never smelt before.

The woman's arms are around me and then the door is opened. The sky is so nearby.

We roll in the grass; drinking in the rich fragrance of it. The ships squat over the veldt like silver mantises.

I will not bow nor dream; not yet; if I should find the thing who will kill my enemies I'll seize it, here in this beautiful place.

64.

Whose vast heart, remnant in the leaves and houses, sculpts for us the edged brow of the land, cut into by the wind and water, regnant and singular underneath the order of the stilted cart stars:

Too impassioned for words. The block, scene and script written onto our mast, man woman and boy; keeled to the moor and nameless in it, novice explorers of an ocean we cannot name either.

She's crying, and I hold her against my chest, knowing whose raiment this is; part of our own.

It's a call to will with poison what I must do; something I don't even know yet but which I can feel in my gut like the old dreams, from my old life, before this one.

How many lives can one body live? I think they're measured by feelings, peaks into valleys, but one cannot go back.

- -

"What do we do now?" she asks me.

"Where are we?" says the boy.

I can no longer remember their names; but I love them.

"Let's be patient. I saw some food in the ship. Are you hungry?"

It's a strange kind of bread, bland but filling. The boy eats eagerly, crumbs spilling from his mouth.

"Isn't it beautiful," I say. The woman nods, her

eyes squinted against the light.

The man appears from behind one of the trees and we all stand silent, catching our breaths.

He shines brightly in the light; perhaps he is made of metal. But his smile appears human.

No burning mast; no fire, no radiation or thought of divinity; no purchase nor chance of any; not any reason nor rendition of reasons, no ballads of gatekeepers sullen and shameless riddled with answers and faded into newswax; not jumping for joy nor named in the poem to recite with glory and stars—he whose choice binds us more deeply, you in the gutter, made elsewhere but changed there, in the gutter:

Not the death of the kingdom; not even revolution; it is instead a stopping of that turning.

Stop the world; ease it closer to the edge.

We're going to get off.

No lance and light; no pillar of fire or salt; no voice from the sky.

He whose messages are ignorant and wise; shuffled under his feet; stomped and paraded in silence; godawful poems written onto bark, illegible, illegible leaflets, screaming mute in illegible leaflets, he whose arbiter is time; tick and tock; chumming and mumbling over the fire; one and then the other, and then the other; marching over the rancid flames to deliver the news:

65.

Though we conduct ourselves by day it is at night that our cerements and shelves of selves do the hidden work, underneath our feet and underneath our eyelids, for the homecoming of the spirit:

Each day hidden away underneath our abattoirs and masonries, underneath our children's games and county lakes far come and designed, underneath our worldly things:

Each hour, limitless in abandon, set to and forward in the desire to come to be, to have at it, to make known the kingdoms invisible to the eyes of Man, Woman, or Child, our night-workers tie up their sheaves for the harvest:

Time them up; over your shoulder; up in the air.

Whosoever craves meaning fills their work: night worker work. To see how it is when you are gone, before you are, and to see how it is that these things we made are still here, still coming back, and ready for our re-arrival, over the spirit and the hands of men.

What terrible cathedral is this, our refuge, so that we might be granted a look at the spell of our labor, and a tool to do it with.

I should have known earlier—just how it would come to be. How I would read see the horrible crimes of my people and flee them. But I can't; not in advance. It's not my gift.

"What is he?" she asks me.

"A man."

"He's an angel!" said the boy.

"Maybe."

The man came and pointed at the bread and I gave him some. He sat with us, eating. His metal face shone like a lantern.

What would I have done if I had known. Would I have done better? Been better? Perhaps I would have been even more afraid.

We've gone in the lake. Me, the metal man, woman and boy. I don't know any of their names, including mine. But I know who we are.

66.

We're not alive, not quite. We're dreaming, or something like it. Meditating, hibernating, hovering under sleep. Not quite alive, not yet, where we hum in the deep, in the deep black news who keeps coming round, of my homecoming in the shadowed land of blood bone and sickness, where the farmers come to die, and I help them, or helped them, in my youth.

Am I still young then? Am I old? Middle-aged. Like Middle Earth, Mediterranean, always inadequate, too tightly circumscribed, held in held on held tough waiting for the right moment to appear:

They're all around me glimmering in the water. I could get up, I could say something. Wake us up out of this spell; but it's too beautiful. Water and day and approaching night over the green trees.

The worlds press together in me; but that doesn't matter. When didn't they?

The work of killing I must do; that I have done. What is the escape from it?

67.

In the signal to noise ratio, ultimately we must determine how much noise we want. That is, how many signals are we willing to perceive simultaneously? There's nothing without a signal. Everything is signaling everything else.

To move reality, beneath your feet, under your arms, over your hair, in your sleep, around your head, on your hands, in your teeth and set in mounds about you, shaped into the world:

To take command.

Arbiter. Accept your staff.

Like the musical staff. Carved into wood. Set the movement into the world, and beat its coming under your thumb.

But whose drum am I beating?

What is this noise in the air?

What religion is this, who makes my hands and face; who tells me I am here; doing these things; making music with my weary heart.

Whose height and mast do I feel trembling beneath me; whose shade is the earth who takes so many colors, over what distance and name; black and midnight carried onion black and rhymes, shapeless and feeling, numberless black rhymes feeding my burden pushing me in:

Over and in.

Command.

Over the bark and beetle to the brush edge of

the canvas, master:

68.

Well. We're returning. It shouldn't have been so soon but there it is. Up and over and into the ship. The woman and boy are upset; they want to stay. But there is no life for us here. And now we have our friend, who I have named . . . well, never mind his name. Likely I will forget it soon anyhow.

Now the ship is under my command. No other officers are aboard.

"Are you ready?" I ask them. And they nod. My friend is standing near, and I close my eyes.

We're returning through the well. We're coming up.

We're coming closer to what this thing is. What is this thing, who we have named and own, and which owns us? This thing, who I have named freedom, this evil thing, given to us to do our work, whatever we decide it to be, but whose passage into the world creates its own insistences, inertia.

We begin and don't stop.

I will stop it but I am afraid.

Counting down. One. In the dark. Two. In the light. Three, twilight masts and faces. Four, in the blue water.

Come over my blue water, where I have lain barren, and be ready for my kiss, who is not so bad, but will make you feel you have been dead, and may yet revive. Come out of death with me, whose shadow is still as a bird, to see who it is we are and whose mane we've stuck onto our face, priapic and blasted, cursed warrior with no war, magus arcane splintered mad, wandering over the earth and beyond, pitiful bird. Flightless.

Five. We're home.

69.

"Stay with the Somalians. I should have told you to stay there the first time."

"What will you do?" she asks me. "And what if they find us there?"

"You'll be safer there than with me."

"I'm coming with you."

"You should stay with the boy. He has no one else."

"He has you."

"I want you both to stay safe. At least I will have done that."

"Who do you think you are that you can command us like some general? You're just a traitor who we decided to follow. And now you would betray us again?"

"No, I wouldn't do that."

"Take us with you."

70.

The superweapon is part of the problem. That thing which can defeat the insurmountable power obviously becomes it.

Even if I have no intention of becoming the child-eater who I mean to kill, there are other problems.

If I use this ship and blast their temple into ruins; hunt them into the furthest caves, burn them out and slay them, if I destroy their ways and keep alive the memory of them; but doing it with this weapon—isn't it a mistake?

But what else can I do? I have no army.

And there is another problem: what if the priests were right, and these aliens are the true masters? How can I imagine than I am given this gift in innocence? They are not innocent. They may well imagine some worse fate for us and I walk into it so faithfully—ridiculous.

I am a ridiculous man on a ridiculous quest. You might as well say I am out to slaughter every last man, ending with myself. To change our spirit.

I don't know.

But I will do it.

71.

Name the thing and we'll be saved; but salvation is furthest from my mind. It's always the problem: embark on your quest only to discover you had been asking the wrong questions and are looking for the wrong thing entirely. But once started, one cannot return.

You can only change where you're going.

Our friend is completely silent but he does help row. Row row row your boat, gently up the stream, merrily merrily merrily merrily life is . . .

. . . this thing, made out of dough. Not yet baked. Still rising:

The question as always is how much do I want to remember. If I remember too much, will it endanger my mission? How much did I permit to happen. What does it mean that I rebelled? If that is what I did.

It doesn't matter. I am aboard. With my friends.

I hold her hand and the robot man rows; and I close my eyes to listen to the waves.

72.

Stroke. Under the sky. Stroke. The air at night a sleeve of dream; shivered delight and doors down into our kingdom beneath.

Stroke. The horizon hints at red—just barely—the lightest touch, as my own body is the lightest touch, barely hinted. Only here by accident, and given all manner of powers, reasons and events to wrap my hands around, and pull—

I fear not what our friend is capable of but what I am. That is what power is—simply the future. Future collapsing into now in full color, dazzling and dancing around one, asking:

Just what is it that you want, my son? And what are you willing to do to get it?

73.

"What can you do?" I asked him.

In my mind I saw the image of flowering heat; energy streaming out of his head.

"How much can you do it?"

He just kept rowing.

"What else can you do?"

He looked at me then and I understood I had made a mistake; or rather, understood again. I was not the man for this—I was too weak. And he knew it.

"Well, it will have to be enough."

- -

Whose grievous reign has been mine; my people's. Whose bitter melons and years made ours know what the dregs were to come; and which doors would then be opened. What elusive god made my name and my family's, bitter as peat, and as black, streaming out of the ground as some hateful ichor. What is it? Nothing at all?

I fear it isn't; that it is a piece in this thing I have tumbled into—entirely expected, perhaps even necessary. Yet this is the same sophistry I always despised in the priesthood; this notion that horrendous suffering is somehow necessary. That our cruelties are endorsed by this universe.

Perhaps not endorsed but expected. And having begun them, we're entitled to see what otherworldly fruits they bear.

What black grail so near; righteous and unafraid; article and inhabitant, huge over the storm, alive: whose weight and shift the strip and kick prickling my spine; whose stone and ash what fatal hand, the mercury and night, escorting me over the dark:

What black grail dispels these deeper myths; onomatopoetic; illustrious brine; drink of the damned. Give it me and I will drink; I hope it is fatal poison.

Who is it we're coming to?

What grosser symphony of the gods, arbiter of justice, enactor of treaties and disease; magistrate over the harbinger of death, singing in your ear:

Whose majesty inscribes the night with our dreams, flashing our spirits with this divorce, all mansions crumbled and steeping into the plain of thought:

Which canyon do you invest in us, black keeper, and malevolent deity, haunting our days with your sweet voice, whose might is our launching slow and unfearful into the vast depths of your arms, uninterruptible, clawing our gap across the pace of our hearts, gowned and ready, bride to the deep, plastic forks and microwaved dinners held tight before the gaze of the television, in every color known to Man, and Woman.

What grave symphony bought from children, selling roses in clay vases, spiral painted, moves over the earth, casting us our lights, red and viscous alone, descending:

What maniacal king, bent into the heap of his tragedy, invites us here to make our shelter, wilted and crying, making of the ash of the year our necklaces and charms, icons and epics, populating the raging vortices stories through ten thousand generations—what face, clinging to the mask of our own, rigid and unmoving, unable to speak, nor see; clover covered sweltering body, rising to meet us in the mine:

What's mine and yours, what's mine is mine, yours is yours, in the mine, graving our robbers to speak to us; tell me, what did you take? Was it good? I want to touch it again, so I can remember who I was that day, when I held my weapon for the last time, then went to work again;

the pageantry of our gaoler, step to step, majestic, iron and sad, waiting for his ale, watching us through the bars, his fate in the hours and centuries of keeping us beneath the ground: what lion, dead too long, numbs our faces for this resurrection into our bounty, into our comeuppance, no sword nor mayor not even any dream but the feeling of light; the first we have ever seen in this life; noxious and discolored but light; rocking us awake, out of our barnyards and crèches, whimsical mad:

to summon you to our perusal of your neck this close;

and closer;

what is it we feel is ours, your slaves, come to your death; the winter gone; but summer not able to be spoken, fled perhaps, into our steps away;

what is the thing we have forgotten, in our movement again round you, copper knife in hand, to make you ours, deeper into yours, our man, named and bewildered but ours, locked again into our bog to descend, knife to throat.

Who made us to you, lyrical divide of the flesh from man, and your words to our sky, not eligible to be ripped from the womb of the stars as you claim, but sent again to labor in your grave, digging and digging again to find who it was we thought we had hurt, who it was he believed we had punished in our own, again.

Whose reaper is in us come to kill; rich and sweet; eager and taloned; hearing our only love to separate our future from your eyes.

74.

Often the hardest thing is believing. Not in god—I don't care about that—but in the world.

"If we succeed, what will we do then?" I ask her.

"Whatever we want."

"What do you want to do?"

"I want to take a bath."

The sun stands indecent above us, watching our approach into Ma'amir.

"What will you do, boy?" I ask him.

"I don't know."

"What do you want to do?"

"I want to sleep in the mountains. And watch the stars."

"We can do that."

I pay the harbormaster to take no note of us. Part of the fee is our raft.

North again. We have covered our friend's face in a cloak; he has arresting eyes.

75.

This deep and desperate hunger: what does it arise from? How did it move my ancestors to behave as they did, leaving behind the life of the land to enter into the abomination that is our birthright? Was it only a matter of degrees? Or was it a cataclysm?

Why did they surrender to it? Surely they knew it to be madness. And why do I have to keep asking? The answers do not matter. All that matters is what we do now.

- -

The dare in the day; my heart; when will it be easy for me? To know that I am doing, if not the right thing, then at least something which has a reasonable chance of success. The world never made any sense to me to begin with, but it has only made less sense over time. And at the same time I marvel at it, also more as I age. I find it only more amazing.

Perhaps that is one of the functions of death: this respite from amazement, in a final surfeit of it. We can only handle so much.

Grave of my family, future love; let me tell you the tale of the days gone by, whose nearness was a great grief and happiness to me, in the days before I learned to forget.

Whose name I use is yours; I could use no other. We're bound in destiny by the stars, but more by one another, unable to forget one another's faces, though I have forgotten your name many times.

The name I use is history; the burial raft of our people; burning high in the imagination; the smoke is fine and you can see it for some distance, over the valley.

Which name I use is unimportant though. I only want to say that I am grateful for the chance to tell you; whatever it is I am able to. Soon the chance will be taken from me. But before it is, know that I loved you, nameless wanderer in the dark.

The burial raft is deep and high; and I can feel his cousin moving over the rafters, peeking down.

Here is his eye, the sun. And my adopted son.

Light before dusk.

76.

We think we know what we're doing but it's a charade; which is itself useful information. Inside the charade our actions encode a monolith not entirely out of our control; etching around the edges of the fabric, little rhizomes, intent on their duty to the stone:

The moon is above us as we walk.

"How far away can you do it, man?" I ask him.

He points to the bush thirty yards distant.

"Good."

Falling away from us the moon fills me with desire, the desire for both death and knowledge; running my hamster wheel to my interior burn point.

I have to decide how to use this weapon, who is also a man.

"How shall I use you, man?" I ask him.

I see the red door in his mind.

"What is it?"

A sun.

"What does it mean?"

He looks at me; like always he says nothing. His eyes are flat, and heavy.

"Are you tired?" I ask the woman and the boy.

They say nothing also.

I feel I have condemned us all to death.

77.

What burns in me is not a man; I don't know what it is.

Is the law a thing of men? I thought justice meant separation, as a judge separates the guilty from the innocent. But perhaps it is some more ancient thing, as among some tribes the word for law is the same for marriage and the verb "to go."

To go into marriage is the law; or simply going.

I should marry the woman and adopt the boy.

"I'll be your father if you want me to, boy," I tell him.

"Thank you," he says, and I hold his hand.

"Shall we camp on the hill? You wanted to see the stars."

"Yes."

78.

Some might condemn me as a heathen for seeking to destroy that which I do not understand. But what is there to understand about child eating? Is it any different from the madman who mutilates his body in a rage, under the moon?

As children are our own body.

I don't need to understand it. Only destroy it.

ORPHAN HOLD
DO NOT SHIP

H1 – 000000000247

ISBN 9781940830308

CLIENT	Alternate Sourcing
STATION	TPP Receiving Station 03
HELD	2026 – 10 – 08 08:49

SHELF

If its order arrives, scan this label at a receiving station.

79.

I can almost see where I am going. Part of it is in the boy's eyes. But part of it is in an absence in the woman's—she has been more colored by the city than me. I am surprised she came with me at all. Perhaps she is a spy. Perhaps she regrets her decision. Or both, and more. Aren't all woman spies of a kind? Always looking for the next opportunity.

Who I wrote is dead; the man I remembered being. That is not quite right, but I don't know the word for it. A life I might have lived, but am no longer sure. He is dead in the sense of a friend who you no longer talk to, and so surely must no longer be your friend, but you have not checked, and are probably afraid to.

I am dead also, but am reviving. Corpse out of the ground. I have my hand on the edge of the grave, and am looking for purchase, to boost myself up.

I want to burn it up; burn up every scrap of my heritage. Bury my city in the ground and forget it ever existed.

80.

The nobility in me is poison but it will not out; for it means known, and this thing will not descend nor be misremembered. It cannot escape.

No empire can descend, for it has been laid out, sheer as a cavalcade of knives, each hour and minute arranged so as to parade our vengeance over the land, and one another.

No splendor can unite us, but it will only grow more beautiful. Over the night air I have seen our solemn wind, descend into the valleys of our bodies, there to rest for our divination, into what we're going to be:

81.

The chief problem—over and above the immediate one of penetrating our temple, assassinating the high priests, and their allies—is what will happen once I have liberated our slaves.

And who, unbeknownst to me, remains allegiant to the slavers.

I can't scatter my people to the winds. Though we may not remain at Gobekli Tepe I am beginning to suspect.

I am theirs, despite everything.

- -

Gobekli Tepe lies atop a slow-rise hill, a modest looking stone altar, at the center of our wheat and chickpeas. The main complex is underground.

I stand under the trees with my man, woman and boy. I have forgotten my own name too but none of that is important: the moon is important. It is too bright.

"We've arrived too early," I whisper.

"No, we haven't," he says. His voice sounds like rocks tumbling in a stream.

He rises then over the trees, like mist from the river.

I follow behind him, just a pony on a leash. My woman and boy come also.

The guards are asleep.

We descend behind our man into the vestibule.

The stone face of Melek Taus, defier of the

gods, rises above us in the lower entrance.

My man's dark eyes watch me.

I take out my knife and descend to the next level.

"You! Who is it!"

It is my old teacher, Vahit. He stands over the second altar, reading entrails.

I can feel my breathing quicken. I do not answer him but approach the altar.

Behind me I can feel my man; Vahit does not seem to notice him.

"Vahit," I say.

"Deerblack, come and help me. My assistant is sick. What do you see here."

I cross to the altar; he has arrayed the chicken guts across it, his hands inside them like a cook, kneading meat.

"My augury is rusty, Vahit."

"Come, come, you see here, under the heart? What does it look like to you?"

"A face, lord."

"Yes! What kind of face?"

"I don't know. I've brought my friends with me; I must speak to you."

"Yes, yes. Come, look at the face. What do you see in it?'

"It is an evil face, lord. A cruel one. Hungry."

"Is that what you see? I hadn't thought of that. Disturbing."

"We're here to free the prisoners, Vahit. My man here will ensure that this happens."

"Yes, he looks serious." Vahit smiled. "There's some of the bird left. Why don't I feed you travelers?"

"All right."

Vahit spread the remains of the bird's flesh over his skittle and squats by his fire, poking at it.

"Here, the temple is yours. Sit."

"I'll remain standing, lord. My friends will sit with you, if they wish."

"I'll stand with you, father," says my boy.

"He's yours, is he? I recognize your face, boy."

"I thought about killing you, Vahit. I will kill most of the priesthood."

"Yes. Well, the chicken is almost done. The fire is hot!"

My man's face is like Melek Taus: impassive.

"Will you eat?" I ask him. He nods slightly, and I hand him some of the meat.

I eat too; that I might disgorge myself of whatever offerings I afforded this place, though I know it is impossible. Absurd for me to have done any of what I have, I suppose. Perhaps I should trust myself more.

- -

Who heard death, firm cloak of my body, the awful pell of it, like another world, so close to their own, whose mane and laps circle around my face, ordering my rebirth; I wish I knew who made them this way; if I could speak their language, know what they're saying.

The wakefulness of it needs getting used to; that I'm bound to it.

Like to a drug.

Ten hours till surfacing:

- -

Only under the water, where I remember—where I'm safe—who made the world this way. That I should remember so much, but be unable to do anything about it. What sort of logic is that? Ridiculous.

- -

"What do you think you were doing old man?" I take him by the throat.

He begins to choke on his chicken.

I press in on his throat with my thumb.

"Was he one of the ones who hurt you, son?"

He shakes his head. I let up the pressure on my thumb.

"You're going to watch your temple destroyed," I tell him. I take my hand off his neck. He puts his hand over his reddened flesh, watching me with frightened eyes.

I take hold of his arm. "Take me below."

82.

Who heard me cry, in the night. Who dealt me the card, triumphant, avenger, locked leering and made iron; made enraged.

The orgy is already underway; the priests and their boys.

I take the first's head in my arms, and press my knife against and through his neck. My alien friend has taken another, lifting the bearded thing like a sack of laundry, and breaking the skull against the wall. I move to the next and from my friend's eyes come stars, swirling over the priests' faces, burning their skin.

I shove my knife into his heart. And then the next.

Who heard me reckoning with the times over my heart, no nearer shelter, nor so very far away, lamplight and thick, the sound of doves, like the ones I would sacrifice, and the sound of the boys, crying like lambs at the slaughter.

I strip the clothes from Vahit and force him to his knees.

"Apologize to these boys. Tell them why we will destroy this temple."

"It was Melek Taus' decision," the old man begins, and I take my knife back against his throat.

"Don't lie to them!"

"I'm sorry boys," he says with wide eyes. "As our brother Deerblack says, it's time to move on. I

. . . I'm sorry for what I did to you."

The boys become enraged then, piling around him like hounds around a kill.

I take my man's arm. "Let us get them some clothes."

83.

Gobekli Tepe, Potbelly Hill; the problem has already arrived and I am it; one of them; the man with the gut pressed underneath my ribs, and over my waist. Our mark of the man, created by wheat.

It was wheat which made the pot belly, and our hill. As it made our skin. What does it mean? And is there some way to escape it?

What have I done? And what have I been doing all these years?

It is too tempting to say it was only a few bad actors; only a handful of sinners. Then we could kill them as I have done and be rid of it. What we have made is deeper than a few high priests. Even destroying the temple will not be enough; I do not know what will be.

Still, it is good to do. We've set fire to the rooms and buried our ancestral bones along with the animals; filling every room.

Charnel house of charnel houses, burning.

The smoking wreck delights me and the boy; I hold his hand and tell him about our future in Europe.

84.

Whose ash is my face; winter and rain and the sun, our pilgrimage a cut through the rusted hulk of the thing who is our memory; burning not behind us but within, like the chicken in my stomach.

Who, black as my face, must I endeavor to understand, as I move from my victory into our deeper heartache, of the past creeping over our future, like water from rain soaking my socks.

"I'm sorry, boy," I tell him.

"Don't you remember my name?"

"No. What is it?"

"It's Jacob."

"We'll call you James."

85.

What black grail so near; righteous and unafraid; article and inhabitant, huge over the storm, alive: whose weight and shift the strip and kick prickling my spine; whose stone and ash what fatal hand, the mercury and night, escorting me over the dark:

What black name, like my son, grips my body in deliverance:

About the author

Robin Wyatt Dunn was born in Wyoming in 1979. You can read more of his work at www.robindunn.com.